GERTRUDE'S SWEETHEART

MONOLOGUES FOR READERS AND ACTORS

GERTRUDE'S SWEETHEART

MONOLOGUES FOR READERS AND ACTORS

EDITED

BY

BART MEEHAN

ArtSound Press

Canberra

ArtSound Press
Canberra, Australia
Website: ArtSound.fm
Contact: ArtSoundtheatre@gmail.com

First published in Canberra, Australia by ArtSound Press 2024

Cover art by Trish Dillon

PERFORMANCE RIGHTS

These monologues are free for use in auditions, as well as amateur or school productions. Permission of the copyright holder is required for any professional performance, broadcast or reproduction. Enquiries can be directed to:artsoundtheatre@gmail.com or bart.meehan@gmail.com

Printed and bound by Ingram Sparks

ISBN: 978-0-6457692-2-7 (Paperback)

For me, the monologue was the favourite thing I had done in radio. It was based on writing, but in the end it was radio, it was standing up and leaning forward into the dark and talking, letting words come out of you.

Garrison Keillor

Actor Denzel Washington once said *(my paraphrasing)* there is no such thing as a monologue, that even if it is only you on stage, you're still talking to somebody sitting out there in the darkness. The thoughts you are externalising are part of a moment you are having with the audience.

For me, the monologue is the most intimate of theatrical experiences, allowing you, (as writer Norman Lock says), " to be inside one's character, to register his or her every vagrant thought, emotion, and response - the first-person viewpoint grants this privilege and immediacy."

In this small collection you will find monologues that give you that "first-person viewpoint". They were written to be performed, and all have been brought to life on stage and radio (as part of the ArtSound Radio Theatre program broadcast on ArtSound FM, Canberra) but they are more than performance pieces. They are stories ... of love and loneliness, humour and heartbreak, ego and eccentricity...and they are a joy to read because in some way the challenges faced by the disparate group of characters you are about to meet, echo in our own lives.

So if you are a reader, find a quiet spot and turn the page. And if you're an actor, stand up at the family dinner and deliver one of the stories you'll find here...

Bart Meehan

TABLE OF CONTENTS

GERTRUDE'S SWEETHEART

Kirsty Budding

(Male, 70+)

I met Gertrude at the bingo. She'd lost her glasses and couldn't see her numbers. I was the lucky man who got to help her guide her pen. Every time my hand brushed hers, she giggled like a sixteen-year-old. Made me forget I was in a retirement home. I was so happy; I couldn't bring myself to tell her that her glasses had been on her head the whole time.

The next morning, I walked down to the corner shop to buy her some flowers. I thought of her giggle every step of the way. But by the time I got back to the residents' lounge, the seat next to her was taken. It was Mr Willoughby – that smooth-talking Lothario from 29a. He's a retired British officer who wears a tweed suit and has the straightest back I've ever seen. Hardly any arthritis. He sounds like David Attenborough and he can dance – not just a slow dance; he can do the twist, the jitterbug, the tango.

He's next to Gertrude telling jokes and she's giggling away, saying, "Oh Mr Willoughby, you are funny!"

Cad. (*Confiding a secret*) Last year, there was a scandal involving Willoughby and Mrs Smith from 28a. That's right: *Mrs* Smith. Mr Smith was in the rehabilitation wing recovering from a hip replacement and Willoughby was ready to provide comfort, if you get my meaning. No one was surprised when Mrs Smith died of a heart attack; it was the most action she'd had in thirty years.

Then there was Mavis. And Betsy. And Doris. All decided they wanted a happy ending. I tell you: with Willoughby around, "assisted dying" has taken on a whole new meaning.

And now he was after my Gertrude! Well, when I was young, I'd have walked away. But I'm old enough to know if you love someone then you should just bloody tell them. I wasn't going to let him take her back to his parlour without a fight! So I shuffled over, holding my flowers like a schoolboy, and I said:

"Gertrude. I'm old and I can't dance and it took me an hour to get you these flowers from the corner shop, which is 400 metres away. I have a crooked back and I don't sound like I narrate nature documentaries for the BBC, but I love you."

"I can also assure you that your life expectancy will be significantly higher if you choose me. So, if you want a few minutes of excitement followed by a heart attack, then Willoughby's your man. But if you want someone who will wear you down gradually over a number of years before you finally die peacefully in your sleep, then take these flowers, and be my sweetheart."

Willoughby sneered, but Gertrude giggled and took the flowers. Then she took my arm – and as we left the lounge like two teenagers off to the pictures, she whispered:

"I knew the glasses were on my head."

GIVE ME GRANDCHILDREN

Kirsty Budding

(Female, 50+)

Sit yourself down! It's been weeks; why do you never visit your mother? Always working, working. Cup of tea? Are you hungry? Are you sure? You're looking thin. Are you ill? Look at those skinny hips. Need to get some meat on your bones!

How's Jonathon? Still doing a PhP? Sorry, PhD. What's it in again? Oh, that's right, poetry. That'll get him a good job won't it! (*laughs*) So what's his job going to be, a Doctor of Poetry? Just make sure he doesn't get up on an aeroplane when they ask if there's a doctor on board! Not the same thing, is it. Because one's useful.

Your father came up with a cracker yesterday! Do you want to hear it? What's the difference between a PhD in poetry and a roast chicken? ... One feeds a family! (*Laughs*)

(*Suddenly serious*) You do want a family, don't you. Because you know I've been knitting baby clothes since you were twenty-five. Obviously that was some years ago so I had to expand to toddler clothes, and then school-age clothes. I've just finished the year six range.

I don't know the gender but I've been assuming it will be a girl… you know, because of Jonathon. But I've done the odd blue thing just in case you have the boy first and the girl second. Two children: a boy and a girl. A pigeon pair! Can't have one child: they get spoilt, or strange. Can't have three or four: then you can't buy the family pass at theme parks. And we'll need that when your father and I take them to Disney Land.

Did you know that fertility declines rapidly in your thirties? I'm not pressuring you darling! I just want you to be aware that every day, your eggs are going stale. You know how your father sometimes forgets to put the milk back in the fridge and then it goes all lumpy? That's what's happening to your ovaries. Take my advice: put a few in the freezer while they're still fresh.

Speaking of which, I've got a nice casserole defrosting in the kitchen. You are staying for dinner, aren't you?

AUNTY AUSTEN

Kirsty Budding

(Female, 40+)

My dear madam,

It is a truth universally acknowledged that, no matter how accomplished a lady is, when she is trying to decide whether she should break up with her boyfriend, she will Google it.

This truth is so well-fixed in Google's algorithms that Google knows the question before the lady has finished typing it. She need only type 'should I b' – just the letter b – before she sees the following options in order of popularity:

Should I break up with my boyfriend?

Should I buy a mac?

Should I buy a house?

Hello, I'm Jane Austen. You may remember me as the author of such classic literary hits as *Pride and Prejudice, Sense and Sensibility,* and to a lesser extent, all of the other novels I wrote.

Although I never married and the concept of a carnal relationship outside of marriage is unpalatable to my late 18th to early 19th century sensibilities, I am here to save you from the Wickhams and Willoughbys of the 21st century.

Let us begin. Ahem.

Obviously you should break up with him because you are asking Google. This is a clear indication that you know the answer, but you do not trust yourself. I understand it is usual for ladies in these situations to seek advice or to create a "pros and cons" list, for example: *Pros*: we both enjoy reading, dancing and playing the pianoforte. *Con*: when he touches me, I feel nothing, as if my lady flower has shrivelled up and died.

As I have often noted, a marriage without passion cannot be agreeable to either party. The thought makes me more depressed than the casting of Keira Knightly as Elizabeth Bennet in *Pride and Prejudice,* when Jennifer Ehle clearly defined the role in the 1995 BBC adaptation.

Of course, it is possible that the lack of physical attraction is mutual and that this is acceptable to both parties, in which case you may simply be elderly or infirm.

However, if you lack amatory inspiration, try roleplay. (*Imitates sexy roleplay voices*) "Oh Mr Darcy! / Oh Lizzy! / You are tolerable I suppose, but— / Oh shut up and take me!"

(*Regains composure*) Let me advise you that writing a pros and cons list is quite foolish for, as I demonstrated in Mr Collins' hopeless proposal to Lizzy, love is not a business proposition. A lady who is truly in love would never dream of listing the cons of her soul mate.

Perhaps he is cruel or dishonourable; perhaps he is proud, or even prejudiced. Or perhaps he is perfectly agreeable, but he is just not your Mr Darcy.

It is not his fault, and you cannot explain why, but you know in your heart that something is missing. You fantasise about a room of one's own. Independence! Freedom!

I never married, though I had *many* chances... alright I only had one chance. But still, if I had married, I would not have had time to write. I may even have died in childbirth at a young age, instead of reaching the ripe old age of thirty-seven.

If I had married my own Mr. Darcy, I would not have been able to write some of the most popular and adored works of English literature. My refusal to conform has led to generations of people remembering my name, while my contemporaries are forgotten.

My dear madam, perhaps you are destined for greater things than simply marrying Mr. Darcy.

Your role model,

Jane Austen

Postscript. You should not buy a mac. They are most displeasing.

Post-Postscript. It is excellent that ladies are now able to own property. You should purchase an estate if the conditions are favourable, to wit: a good-sized deposit, reasonable interest, and a positive forecast for growth. Otherwise, you will have no assets when you are an old spinster, and you will be forced to enter a workhouse.

LET ME PLAY THE LION TOO

John Lombard

(Male, 30+)

The great actors are defined by their versatility.

I think of Alec Guinness in Kind Hearts and Coronets, bringing to life a family of nine distinct characters. I remember Lon Chaney, the silent film era's Man of a Thousand Faces, transforming himself with only make-up, wires and putty into the Phantom of the Opera and the Hunchback of Notre Dame. More recently, I was moved by Scarlett Johansson's defiant plea that she be allowed to play any person, or any tree, or any animal she wishes. Bravo!

As an actor, I understand this yearning only too well. It is rapture to capture the belief of an audience with a fine performance. The satisfaction is only greater when you master a challenging role. Like Bottom in The Dream, I would be Pyramus, and Thisbe, and moon, and wall, and lion too. Oh, to incarnate every part! That is the actor's ambition!

As an actor that can shape-shift, I have been blessed to tackle a staggering array of roles. Able to mold my body into any form, I can never be typecast. To my knowledge, I am the only actor to have played both Scout and Atticus in To Kill A Mockingbird, all three witches in Macbeth, and the dog in Old Yeller. I have been both Romeo and Juliet, and one magical night infiltrated the chorus of Hamilton.

But as every actor knows, ours is a calling, but not always a living. Many of us supplement our vocation with mundane jobs, whether it be washing dishes or stamping paperwork. I am no different. I may rob banks, but not from greed. My larceny funds the creation of the greatest art of them all: live theatre.

In recognition of these criminal endeavours, I recently found myself nominated for inclusion in the FBI's Most Wanted list. Although celebrity is always an honour, this interest from the authorities forced me to court a lower profile. Therefore, I took to incognito performance in humbler venues than I am used to, including community theatre.

Now, I do not consider myself above community theatre, despite my extensive professional experience. An actor with humility may draw profound satisfaction from amateur theatricals. For instance, my performance as Blanche in the Lower Franklin

County Players production of A Street Car Named Desire was praised as "bold" and "unconventional" in that community's respected mouthpiece of truth, the Lower Franklin County High School Newsletter. And let me tell you, praise is not lightly given in the arts column of the Lower Franklin County High School Newsletter.

But even rave reviews are not enough to sustain a true artist, and I yearned to realise my dream project: a one man performance of The Grapes of Wrath!

Burning with new resolve, and also perhaps a little frustrated at the unsavoury politics of community theatre, I returned to heists to scrape together seed money. A few inconvenienced insurance companies are a small price to pay for great art.

Unfortunately, the police are too often philistines with misplaced priorities. One night, fleeing from two such representatives of law and order after a botched caper, I found sanctuary in a furniture warehouse.

Considering the recent scrutiny of my nocturnal escapades, I deemed it best to evade these over-enthusiastic censors rather than risk vexatious confrontation. And so, I squeezed my malleable body into a new shape and waited.

The police prowled in helpless confusion, unaware that the leading man had donned the mantle of prop. I had become a couch, indistinguishable from others of the make. By the next day, the search was abandoned.

I intended to stay as a couch only until night, when I could vanish into anonymous darkness. But to my surprise, before then I was lifted by two men and heaved into the back of a truck.

I had been sold. And I was now on my way to my new owner.

Imagine my despair: one of the greatest actors of my generation, deposited in the living room of an ordinary suburban family. As though to mock me, I was placed in front of a tv blaring the incompetent posturing of a daytime soap.

I first met Stephanie, the mother of this family, when she sat on me to try me out. Stephanie was sweet, but a little flaky. Later, she had a nap on me. As a gentleman, I could hardly disturb her.

That night, I met her husband, a sallow and serious man named Mark. I also met their daughter, Maisie, a furtive and sullen teen. Stephanie, Mark and Maisie. This was the Brown family.

Reading between the lines of the family's TV dinner conversation, I observed some fractures. Maisie was skipping school. Mark no longer loved his wife. And Stephanie was sneaking a little more gin than doctors recommend. Here, within this ordinary family, I had found drama worthy of Terence Rattigan or Tennessee Williams! I realised that as a couch I had a unique perch to study these vivid characters!

And so, I embraced this new role as furniture. In the first year of drama school they teach you to move like an animal: how much easier, then, to move like an inanimate object. I created a backstory for myself, from the fabrication of my parts in China through my hasty assembly and successful delivery. I found my intention as this family's hub of comfort, recreation, and connection. When they thrilled to a tense tv program, I was firm as wood. When they sought me for rest, I was fluffy as a cloud. If anyone balanced a bowl of chips on my arm, it would never fall. And beyond all that, I was always preternaturally clean.

I even helped the family out with their lives where I could. Whenever Maisie's sleazy boyfriend sat on me, I flicked him onto the floor. He shortly realised he was unwelcome in our house. And I am proud to say that if coins were dropped between my cushions, they would always be found neatly stacked the next day.

Had Mary Poppins been a couch, she would have been me.

But I am a ham, and as important as the role of couch was, I wanted a richer taste of this family's life. When the house was empty, I became Stephanie, and lived the routine of a mother and housewife. I signed myself up for painting classes, and flirted with my yoga instructor. On other days, I wore Mark's suits and frustrated personality, dashing off plaintive emails to ex-lovers and snotty emails to coworkers. When I found Maisie's secret dope stash, I became an angry teen for an afternoon, getting high in my bed and burning a few holes in my curtains. I loved being the Brown family.

After a time, I was emboldened to grander adventures when the family was asleep. As Maisie, I slipped off to a rave, tried alcohol for the first time, and threw up on my best friend. As Stephanie, my attraction to my yoga instructor became something more, and I began to siphon money from the family's joint bank account. As Mark, I yielded to the frustrations of life and began to cavort in seedy bars, instigating more than one messy fight.

After a few weeks of this character research, I noticed the family had become strangely tense. Suspicion was high with accusations screamed and objects hurled. As a couch I had initially been a source of unity for the family. Now, I sensed that it was time to exit stage left. But first I would have my curtain call.

As so it was that one night, when the family approached me with their tv dinners, I addressed them: a couch still, but with a gaping mouth that spoke hidden truths. I unfurled the family secrets with the showmanship of a confident magician, telling the truth as I had observed and lived it, as all actors strive to.

Only rarely in my career have I had an audience so utterly transfixed. It was impossible bliss!

But they would not see the truth of my character study. Absurdly, they denied their secret shames, and even claimed to love each other. Clods! How could they not see the tragic grandeur of their dark sides?

United, they threatened me with an axe, a bible and a fire extinguisher. This was not the applause I anticipated. I am ashamed to say it, but I lost my temper.

The immortal bard's undying words rang in my mind: "Let me play the lion too. I will roar, that I will do any man's heart good to hear me. I will roar, that I will make the duke say, "Let him roar again. Let him roar again." In my rage, I transformed.

Let me play the lion too!

The Brown family was never seen again. Many newspapers reported on their mysterious disappearance. But only one mentioned the absence of the couch.

Ah, reviews, it is ever thus: the greatest contribution to the drama is always overlooked!

I returned to the Lower Franklin County Players with a new face, nourished by my time as the Browns. Now I would be Shylock or John Proctor or Lady Bracknell. But could I also be a table, a pen or an umbrella? In my hubris, I had narrowed my craft: acting is a wilderness too majestic for the actor to limit themselves to the narrow lives of mere people. Perhaps I am now become the mercurial Puck: an omelette in the morning and a wobbly stool in the evening? I have so much experience to devour!

I'm no Scarlett Johanssen, but I try. Who knows? Perhaps I will be her next. Or a tree, or a rat, or a bat, or a brick!

After all – we great actors are defined by our versatility.

THE LOST HANDKERCHIEF

Harriet Elvin

(Female, 50+)

I found a handkerchief in the street last week.

I was staying down at the coast and doing a bit of shopping – well, we all need to do our bit to support the retailers; it's been very tough the last few years.

I saw the handkerchief in the gutter, looking forlorn.

I looked round - rather furtively - before picking it up.

Now, I don't want you to think I'm the sort of person who'd pick up rubbish from the gutter.

But this wasn't rubbish – it was a neatly folded, lady's handkerchief.

I could see it'd been properly ironed.

Oh, I *do* like an ironed handkerchief!

There's something so wholesome about ironing, isn't there?

I once knew a woman who said a Hail Mary for each pair of knickers she ironed.

She got through a whole decade of the rosary each time she tackled the laundry.

I could never aspire to that standard of piety – or housekeeping, as I draw the line at ironing underwear. But there's something really satisfying about ironing handkerchiefs – simple cotton squares – not difficult at all.

I even sort them into colours before they go back into the drawer.

Sometimes I agonise over whether a white handkerchief with blue flowers should go into the white pile - or the blue pile. And what about one with a pink and green pattern?

I find worrying over these little decisions much easier than thinking about climate change, or rising interest rates, or the situation in the Middle East...

So, I could see from this neatly ironed handkerchief that its owner was a woman after my own heart.

Fine cotton lawn, with a rather old fashioned pink floral pattern.

Apart from being ironed, it gave two other clues about its owner.

On the pink pattern was a bolder stain : a bright red lipstick mark. And it smelled of one of those heavy, classic perfumes : Joy, perhaps, or Chanel No. 5.

And so, I took it – it wasn't *stealing* - it had clearly been lost.

If *I* didn't take it, it really would become rubbish – dirty and wet, swept up next time the council cleaners came through.

I was saving it – this orphan handkerchief.

I would give it a *good home.*

But in taking it I wanted to know its story.

I wanted to imagine the sort of person who'd owned it.

Perhaps it belonged to… to *Janet.*

Janet is one of those large, slightly daunting women : in her late sixties; a rather loud voice; a complexion burnished by the sun. Handsome, in a hearty sort of way.

We all know a Janet. She's the type you find behind the scenes at any community event : setting up stalls; doling out tea from massive urns – *organising.*

If you want something done, ask Janet. She'll help you raise funds for the local bushfire brigade; drive you to a doctor's appointment; look after your children if the babysitter doesn't turn up.

Generous; capable; reliable. That's Janet.

But vulnerable, too. Two years ago, her husband Graham died suddenly. He'd just retired and they'd been planning some travel; more time with the grandchildren; a new kitchen. And all that was snatched away in a moment : he'd had stomach pains, thought it was indigestion, but it wasn't, it was stomach cancer that grew and spread and took over his increasingly frail body and in six weeks it was over and he was dead and Janet was facing life without him.

And Janet felt cheated, robbed of the life they'd planned together.

She was *angry* and perhaps the anger helped with the grief and now, two years later, both emotions are a little dimmed as she's managed to build a life without him.

And today marks one of many new beginnings she's had to embark on, in *"Life After Graham"*.

She's meeting Peter for lunch.

Peter and his wife had been their friends for decades – their children were at school together and they'd kept pace with each other as life passed its various milestones.

Peter's wife died not long after Graham. Since then, Janet's bumped into Peter from time to time : stopped to chat; swapped photos of grandchildren; compared notes on increasing aches and pains : "the organ recital" Peter calls it, with a smile.

There was something there: shared interests…an understanding.

And then he'd invited her to have lunch with him, today, at the smart new café in town.

It was, she supposed, a date.

Janet hasn't gone on a date for nearly fifty years. She doesn't know the rules – what you wear; what you say; what's expected.

She dresses with - for her - unusual care. A skirt's not her thing but she's wearing new tailored pants; a smart blazer.

She checks her image in the bedroom mirror – and has misgivings.

Peter's wife had been one of those fussy, feminine women – twinsets and pearls; nails varnished. Janet regards her own well-scrubbed looks with dismay.

She finds a pretty old handkerchief, not used for many years – man-size tissues are more her style - but clean and neatly pressed.

And here's a bottle of perfume Graham gave her for her birthday, all those years ago in the early married days, before he realised she'd much prefer the latest kitchen appliance.

She sprays it on. It smells foreign and a little exotic.

Deep in the dressing table drawer is a lipstick – given away free with a magazine she'd bought for the knitting patterns.

She smears it uncertainly over her lips – she'd forgotten that coated, rather greasy feeling. A stranger looks back from the mirror, rather accusingly. It's a bit *bright*. But time's moving on and Janet has to go or she'll be late.

Yet, as she parks the car, she has doubts. This new chapter in her life has to be tackled honestly. She takes the handkerchief; rubs the perfume from her wrists; wipes off the lipstick; and in her haste drops it - where it falls to the gutter as Janet dashes off to her lunch date.

Or perhaps the handkerchief belonged to …

… to Stella. Stella is a child of the 1980s but her spiritual home is the 1950s. She yearns for that era of glamour, and femininity.

Stella's home - a modest flat near the town centre - is a retro shrine, her wardrobe a riot of full skirted dresses and tight fitting cardis, accentuating her – rather *generous* - proportions.

In this coastal town she attracts curious looks from the tourists.

But the locals are used to her – she's a lovely girl, with a heart of gold; leads the church choir; clever with a needle; and much in demand for costumes for the local theatre group.

She's got a steady job at a fabric shop where the regulars value her expert advice.

But she feels there could be so much more to life …And today she's on the brink of that so much more.

A new shop is opening in town.

It's called *Vintage Rose* and it's going to sell fifties-era clothes.

Well, not the real thing, you understand, just cheap copies imported from China, but it's a start - and they're looking for a manageress to run it.

It's the *perfect* job for Stella – and today she's being interviewed.

She knows she can make a go of it. She's got the retail experience - and she looks the part.

She'll start small, selling the cheap copies – they're pretty enough to fly off the racks. But over time she'll introduce some real vintage fashions. She'll build it up; buy out the owner; set branches up all along the coast.

She imagines winning a small business award – receiving it from the Mayor of the Shire!

She's got just the outfit for the awards night : a cocktail dress in midnight blue satin –1950s of course.

But first she has to get the job.

She's spent so long choosing the right outfit that she'll be late if she doesn't get moving.

A quick spray of Chanel No. 5 to her wrists; another layer of lipstick; a pretty vintage hankie tucked in her watch-strap – and off she goes.

These heels are not the easiest to walk in and – blast! She's got something in her eye.

She whips out her handbag mirror, removes the grit - but in doing so sees that, in daylight, the lipstick looks – well, a bit obvious – trying a bit hard.

She's forgotten her tissues and there's nothing for it, she'll have to blot the lipstick on her hankie.

She does so and tucks it back in her watch strap, where unseen by her, it floats down to the gutter as she rushes on to her interview.

How did Janet's lunch date go?

And did Stella get that job?

Or did the handkerchief belong to someone else - some other ordinary woman – some *extraordinary* woman – a woman with hopes and dreams, however modest; a woman whose everyday acts of kindness help to weave the fragile webs of our communities?

I washed the handkerchief carefully, removing a stranger's lipstick and perfume.

It lies in my drawer, refreshed and anonymous now; I decided, on balance, it belongs in the *pink* pile.

But handkerchiefs, like umbrellas, are capricious things, easily lost or left behind.

One day it will leave me, too, and move on to other adventures.

SHOPPING FOR UNDERWEAR

Harriet Elvin

(Female, 60+)

It was while I was shopping for underwear for my husband that I first realised the potential for fundamental change in my life.

My husband doesn't need new underwear. Well, to be honest, I don't actually *have* a husband. But, ultimately, these seemed unimportant considerations compared with the profound discovery I made about myself.

It happened like this. On taking early retirement from my job as a senior classics mistress at one of England's better - although not fashionable - private girls' schools, I decided to visit a friend from university days, with whom I'd kept up a dutiful correspondence.

In the annual exchange of Christmas cards, Shirley had invited me many times to visit South Australia, where she and her husband run a small winery in the Barossa Valley. With my retirement, there no longer seemed any valid reason to resist these increasingly pressing invitations.

I decided to stop for a few days in Adelaide before completing the final stage of the journey, both to see the sights of the city and to regain my strength before meeting Shirley. I remembered her as a rather daunting individual, with a loud voice and apparently endless energy.

Afternoon tea at the hotel on my first day was a revelation: I discovered lamingtons and pavlovas - both, I felt, rather more attractive to look at than to taste - and paid with one of those extraordinary coloured banknotes that Australians used as currency.

On my second day in Adelaide, still in that strange, detached state that results from acute jetlag, I wandered out from my hotel on North Terrace and into the retail centre of the city.

I went into a small, rather old-fashioned department store with a vague idea of stocking up with the myriad of small items you inevitably forget in the final throes of packing for a long overseas holiday.

There were signs directing me to departments quite foreign to my experience.

"Men's and women's apparel" intrigued me, with its faintly clinical air.

And so I found myself wandering amongst racks of brightly coloured garments.

"Can I help you?" asked Brian.

I knew his name was Brian from a cheerful badge on his lapel that proclaimed "Hi, I'm Brian!"

I found I was actually in the menswear section, confronted by orderly ranks of shirts and trousers, socks and ties.

Some explanation seemed necessary, and I found myself confiding in Brian that I was shopping for new clothes for my husband, since he himself was a very reluctant shopper.

Something about Brian – his earnest air, perhaps, and sense of vulnerability bestowed by flamboyant acne – trapped me into this lie, and it became increasingly difficult to backtrack.

Feeling a need to explain my English accent, I added we had just arrived for a holiday, and the rather drab selection of clothes my husband had brought with him highlighted the need to refresh his wardrobe.

As I discussed my husband's clothing preferences with Brian, this imaginary creature gained tangible form for me.

He was greying slightly in a way that women's magazines would call "distinguished"; he had a gentle, resigned expression, kind eyes, a faded look.

Now retired, his working life had been one of exemplary - if unexceptional - service, as a family solicitor in a county town, with a solid role in local parish affairs and charitable pursuits.

As to our life together : well, it had been contented, the passion of our early married years distilling into a peaceful companionship.

Grown up children now – grandchildren perhaps.

I forced myself to address the issue in hand, which appeared to be the selection of shirts.

"He'll only wear pure cotton", I told Brian, "or linen, of course – but that's so difficult to iron and always looks so crumpled".

"Awesome" said Brian. What an expression!

I pride myself on being truthful - but now realised how a web of lies could be spun so quickly and how the web, once spun, could be so difficult to unravel.

It appeared necessary to elaborate about my husband. George, I thought, or Henry, perhaps. Yes, Henry – a solid, dependable name.

Of course, it wouldn't go with my surname – Henderson. But then it wouldn't have to, that was the whole point; as a married woman I could leave that name forever.

By now, the selection of clothing for Henry, as I must learn to call him, was starting to grow.

A dark green polo shirt would be perfect for a round of golf at the local club.

A rather brightly striped shirt was, admittedly, more daring than his usual taste, but suitable, I thought, for that Mediterranean cruise we had always promised ourselves one day – or for our trip to the Barossa Valley.

Now that Henry had retired, he had no further use for staid business shirts and ties. He needed something a bit more adventurous.

"He needs new underwear as well", I found myself confessing, rather self-consciously – whether at the increasing complexity of the fiction or from wifely shame, in allowing my husband's underwear to deteriorate to this neglected state.

"No worries," said Brian cheerfully and led me to rows and rows of rather aggressive-looking garments – so unashamed, so male in their unrestrained colours, so thrusting and boldly elasticised, their shape so suggestive of the male form they would cling to.

Resisting the impulse to blush – for this was simply a routine wifely shopping expedition – I regarded the undergarments critically.

“What size does he take?” asked Brian. This, of course, was difficult, but with the confidence of imagination I declared “I’m not really sure, but medium, I suppose”.

“I only wear Bond’s, myself”, said Brian as we discussed make and style.

And I reflected on the incredible nature of context; how it was that I could calmly discuss his underwear with a stranger, someone met only a few minutes before.

As we made a careful selection - I deferred to Brian on such matters as hipsters versus boxer shorts - I reviewed the situation and considered my options.

One : to make some excuse - my wallet left at the hotel perhaps - abandon Brian mid-sale and exit the shop immediately, leaving him to wait, initially hopeful but then frustrated when I failed to return.

The coward's option, of course, but certainly possible.

Two : to explain to Brian that I had enjoyed his company and explanations - but there had been a terrible mistake, as in fact I had no husband and therefore no need of any of the clothes we'd so carefully selected.

Difficult; I'd be demeaned in Brian's eyes, would appear unhinged, and he'd lose any commission he was hoping for on the sale.

Three : I could maintain the fiction and pay for the clothes - after all, with the current exchange rate the cost was modest, and I could put them into one of the charity clothing bins I'd seen further up the road. No doubt someone would be grateful for these new garments.

My fiction could remain intact; my sanity unquestioned; Brian would get his commission; a stranger would be made happy.

Suddenly, the simple recognition that I could quite legitimately buy these items for which I had no use, no purpose at all, revealed a whole myriad of possibilities.

Nobody knew me in this city - I could buy whatever I wanted in this shop. Toys for an imaginary grandchild perhaps; books on home decor for a glamorous lifestyle; lingerie to please an ageing, but still fastidious, lover.

Beyond the heady knowledge of unbounded purchasing power, this realisation of freedom extended across my whole life.

I could stay in this new country of promise and possibilities, and create a new persona and history for myself.

Or I could return to England and forge any one of many futures for myself there.

The realisation of my freedoms and lack of constraints combined with the last traces of jet-lag to give me a pleasant lightheadedness, a sense of mild intoxication.

"Thank you", I said to Brian as I counted out the unfamiliar notes.

"You've helped me today much more than you could know".

SOMETHING HAPPENED

Judith Peterson

(Female, 13 - 17)

Do you ever wonder why you are friends with someone? Like what's a friend anyway... It's like Ali. She wants to be my friend and I sort of hang out with her... I like her but she can be such hard work – things are always about her. What's happening ...how is she feeling...?

Anyway...

This one day... after English... my mum picked me up early to go to an appointment.

We were driving back and I was reading her my English assignment out loud. Actually I was pretending it was in *my* words – I was really reading from a blogger that I like – I wanted to impress her. [*Laugh*]. Anyway, we were driving down around Scrivener Dam – you know the one next to the zoo? I remember looking up to see if I could see the animals - you never can but I like to look... I love the zoo especially the monkeys...

Mum loves telling a story of when I was young and we went to the zoo and we were having hot chips at the kiosk. I was I think 4 years old and I got up and sang a song and the monkeys loved it and jumped up and down in appreciation And then when I finished my song I took a bow and said to the monkeys "thank you, thank you!"

(Giggles then goes sombre…)

Anyway I looked up and this guy caught my attention – he was funny looking... He was walking in a swaying motion – like he had purpose, like he owned the world. He had a beard and thinning hair... He had an army shirt on and jeans with thongs and I thought: " Who wears thongs? Really!"...

Then he got up on the railing of the dam, looked down and put his hands together… like he was praying? Or maybe it was just a dive?

And he jumped. He actually jumped. I am not kidding you, he fuckin' jumped. Sorry about that.

Mum saw it too but she couldn't just stop in the middle of the bridge...like to do something … you know, to stop him. Like how could she? It happened so quickly. She was shocked like me and we were just looking at each other like: "*what just happened*"

So mum stopped at the car park near the bridge and the zoo and I started to call an ambulance but I couldn't talk - so mum took over. Another lady stopped too and she was like: "*did you see that?*" She mouthed it when she came into the car park – she was behind us in her car and saw the whole thing as well I think.

Mum was talking to the police and the girl (Holly was her name) and I were trying to see what had happened. I wanted to see – I wanted to make sure he wasn't dead … but he was...

Mum came over and asked me to get back in the car.

I yelled at her and told her to leave me alone. I was shaken... I was like...I think I just saw a dead guy... OMG OMG.

I was normal - I was like everyone else – and then this happened...

I've heard it said so many times before... but nothing prepares you for seeing something like this... absolutely nothing...

The police came – a really nice guy policeman - *very cute* - with another nice police woman and they asked if I was okay. "

Yeah, I thought, I have just seen a dead guy - a guy jump off a bridge - never been better.

But I said I was okay and then Mum jumped in like a lioness, put her arm, protective you know, around me and said she would look after me to them.

I can still see the police turning up from the other side of the bridge... Running a little then stopping and putting on their gloves and slowly walking up to him. That was when mum asked me to get in the car …a lot firmer this time. And because the cute police officer was there I did what she said...

And then I started thinking - seeing something like that does that to you, makes you think. The thing is, I thought of how I treated Ali that day...

She cuts ... a lot... mainly her legs sometimes her arms. It's horrible - she wears long sleeves even in summer.... Why would you do that to yourself? And there's always a drama with her and her boyfriend. They are so lame.

She says she wants to die like I would say I am hungry... and I think she is so attention seeking and so annoying, but now I think about what happened. If she did something – what *about* if she looks like that guy – I mean dead - I mean *really* dead.

I feel like shit... seeing that guy... not here anymore... dead. I don't want to feel like that - it's the worst feeling....

I think I should message her... I want her to get some help... cause like the way I feel is awful...

(Gets her phone out and messages)

There, I just said I hope she was okay. I know that is so lame but I have to be ready for her shit – maybe I could ask mum for Maccas... I bet she would buy me a large Big Mac Meal cause all this has happened. And a choc frappe... oooh yes that would be great.

Maccas always helps don't you think...?

I could try to be nicer to Ali and to others 'cause you never know how they feel and how maybe your actions could affect that person.

I wonder what was said to that guy that day - or over his life... Its so sad thinking he is gone.

So I will listen to her from now on and keep telling her to get help 'cause I don't know what I am doing – I am only a kid... But I can be kinder and I can watch my words

Like there are services… places she can go like Headspace or at least tell her parents - they could help her more than me... And maybe make sure I say something if I hear something that isn't nice... or people picking on someone... It wouldn't be that hard.. I could do that...

'Cause if something happened…

THE SEAGULL

Bart Meehan

(Female, 70+)

A seagull!

Yes, that's what it'll be. Small and tucked away in a spot where even the White Ladies won't see it.

Ha. How scandalous!

People will look at me and think she's a sweet old thing. They'll say what a lovely granny smile, but they won't know the reason I'm smiling.

But I'll know.

I wonder if it will hurt? I mean they use needles don't they? I wonder if they're sterile?

Oh, don't try to talk yourself out of it, girl! What does it matter at your age!

Besides it couldn't be worse than giving birth to our Sally. She was a great big lump of a thing. Almost ten pounds. I'm not sure what that is in kilos but I do know she didn't want to come out? ...Oh no, she'd have stayed in for another month if I'd let her.

20 hours! That's how long it took. And no drugs.

I mean, if I can go through that what's a little tattoo?

No, the only thing to worry about is whether they can find a bit of canvas without a wrinkle in it.

Ha.

Can you imagine what Bob would have said?

Mind you, he had tattoos himself from his time in the Navy, but he would never have agreed with a woman having one. He was a very conservative, like that.

It's one of the things that drove our Sally mad. She's always been her own woman even when she was a little girl. Bob would say something, another proclamation from the summit, and she'd be disagreeing even before he'd finished a sentence. Very opinionated … just like her father.

They never spoke again after the last big argument. All that yelling and slamming things down on tables and you know, I don't even remember what it was about. Probably some silly political thing. It usually was. But after that, she'd always check he was out before she came over and he'd always call to make sure she was gone before he came home.

I told them they were both being childish, but would they listen?

Of course not! Bob went to his grave thinking he was right and she was wrong. And Sally wouldn't even go to his funeral.

I'm not a hypocrite, Mum

Still, she was a great help afterwards filling in all the paper work and she was brutal clearing out his closet. Not sentimental at all. Everything went in the bins and I'm sure I saw a smile when she threw out his ties. There were so many of them… and they were all blue!

Ha.

For a little while after he'd died, Sally came over to see me every day. She thought I needed the company! It was so annoying but I didn't want to upset her, so I said nothing for weeks. Then, one day over tea and biscuits, I let slip that I quite enjoyed being on my own and she got the hint.

She *is* a smart girl!

Now I only see her every two or three weeks, though she still calls most days. That's fine. I can always say I have something in the oven or there's someone at the door, if it drags on a bit.

You see, I *do* enjoy being on my own after all those years. Having days to myself where I can do what I want.

I can work in the garden, or watch some silly show on the telly without any comments from the end of the sofa. And I'm always using the laptop computer Sally bought me last Christmas. She says its a very good one and it came with six lessons for oldies provided by a pimply boy, in the Rec room at the Seniors Club.

There were 8 of us in that class. All women. Five widows, two divorced and Number 8, Margaret, was a lesbian, which was very exciting. I'd never met one before … or at least I don't think I have.

Margaret told us her partner was all for this computer stuff. Very supportive, she said, which got us thinking that women are probably better at change than men. I mean Bob was still paying for things by cheque until the day he died.

All my old class mates are Facebook friends now, well at least the ones who are still around and I check for new posts from them every morning. There are usually a lot of photos of grandchildren or updates on medical conditions. This morning, one of them said she'd been diagnosed with dementia. She's posted that three times this week.

After that, I *google* the news sites. Bob use to get the newspaper delivered, but it's all on the computer now, so I skim the headlines and then flip over to the obituaries. That's the social page for people my age. It tells you who's in and who's out.

And, of course, that's where I saw his name.

I read the notice twice to be sure, hovering over the age, *84*, and the names of his great grand kids.

Can you believe it? He was a great grand father!

Oh god! Am I really that old?

I thought about going to the funeral for moment, but then decided it would be inappropriate. I mean, his whole family would be there and I wouldn't want them wondering about the strange old women in black, sitting in the last pew.

Besides it was all so long ago…

I wish they'd published a photo of him. It would have been nice to see what he really looked like because in my memory, he's impossibly beautiful.

Wet hair plastered on his shoulders and hard muscles tucked under salty skin. He is *Adonis* standing over me, the sun behind his head giving him a golden crown.

Hey babe, mind if I pull up some sand?

Of course, he doesn't wait for the answer. Just drops his board and settles in next to me. Very close!

Nice bathing suit.

I'd just turned 18 the week before and it was the first time I'd ever worn a bikini. Of course it wasn't like the ones the girls wear today which look like they're made out of shoelaces. My suit had so much material, I could have recycled it as a table cloth. Still it was daring for the time and if my father had known I'd worn it to the beach there would've been a long lecture about what was appropriate behaviour for a young girl…and what wasn't!

What's your name, babe?

Instead of answering I shiver. His voice is rolling over me like honey and depositing words in all the secret places my mother has told me about. Ha.

You cold? Here let me warm you up.

The first move disguised as a concerned cuddle! The second, a light kiss that suddenly turns into deep sea exploration and before I know it he has my tongue pinned down for the count.

I'm surprised at how easily he gets my top off. I don't even feel him unclipping it. But I do feel what happens next, and what happens after that and then after that…

It is glorious!

(*Smiles*)

Well, at least that's the way I want to remember it.

The truth is that it was quick and afterwards there was sand everywhere. I mean everywhere!

Got to catch a wave, babe. See you tomorrow.

And with that he pulls up his shorts, picks up his board and disappears into the sound of the sea.

Wham bam thank you ma'am! That's what they say, isn't it?

Ha ha.

I did comeback the next day and I brought my father's Kodak camera, but he was gone. Moved on to another beach where the waves were better, I suppose.

I wasn't upset. I mean, it was just one one of those wild moments you have in your life. Well in my case...*the* wild moment!

Actually, the only thing I remember thinking was: at least he had the right name for my first man.
Adam.

Ha.

Still, I'd have liked a photograph of him. It would have been my little secret, tucked away at the back of the album.

(*She picks up the album and flicks to a particular page. Looks at it then at the audience.*)

Instead, there's the snapshot of a seagull sitting on some drift wood, with a soggy chip in its beak, that I took on the way home.

No one knows what it means, but that doesn't matter. I do!

THE PURSUIT OF ART

Bart Meehan

(Male, 20+)

There are no small parts, just small actors.

I'm not sure who said that, but it's true. I mean if you're truly dedicated to the craft, you put everything into it.

I was an extra in a commercial a few weeks ago. A face in the crowd behind a guy selling cereal. All I had to do was smile along with everyone else when he hit the pitch line. I could tell they were all just going through the motions… it was another paid gig for them, but I'd spent time developing my character's back story. I knew he was struggling with a new job and that he'd argued with his girlfriend that morning about going to her parents for dinner that night. Her father hated him and never missed an opportunity to point out that he was working his way *down* the ladder of success.

Why was all that important?

Well, it informed the actions of my character. When he smiles after the front man promises the cereal will keep you as regular as clockwork, you can see it's a struggle. His mind really isn't on cures for constipation…he has bigger problems.

And I have to tell you, it worked. When we were finished shooting, the assistant director nodded at me.

He'd noticed.

You see you have to stand out from the crowd in this business.

Like my final exam at College. I decided to do a piece from Hamlet. Not the soliloquy…God, poor old Yorrick has been done to death…no, I decided to do Ophelia's monologue

That unmatch'd form and feature of blown youth
Blasted with ecstasy. / O, woe is me
T' have seen what I have seen, see what I see.

Yes, I know Ophelia was Hamlet's wife. But don't you see, that was the point! Everyone else was doing the Prince...but I took a chance. That's what real artists do.

And I succeeded. *Triumphed*! Our teacher didn't believe in grading creativity. His classes were pass/fail, but when he said *Pass* after my performance, I could hear something else in his voice...it was like he really wanted to say *High Pass,* but couldn't because there were others in the room ...

I winked at him, so he knew I knew.

Of course, I'm not an idiot. I know it'll be a hard road. There are thousands of us out there going for the same parts. That's why my father wanted me to do accounting... so I'd have something to fall back on if it didn't work out. But if you have a safety net you'll never risk anything...and you need *fear* to really make it.

And that's the thing you have to remember, especially when it gets tough...people *do* make it.

I mean look at Tom Cruise. He has a nice smile but he's short and a bit funny looking. That didn't stop him being Top Gun or the guy in Mission Impossible that keeps saving the world.

Well I'm taller and have a nice smile as well…so why not me?

By the way, I did that scene from Risky Business at an audition a while back. You know, the one where Tom's in his underwear singing *Gimme some of that Old time rock'n'roll.* But I did *mine* wearing jocks my Mum gave me for Christmas that have a drawing of a mouse in a tux on the front and "For formal balls only" written underneath.

The director told me it was an "interesting" choice.

No…I didn't get the part, they were looking for someone blonder, but I know he won't forget me. And who knows what might come up in the future.

I heard he's casting a new web series about a zombie rock band called The Grateful Dead. I'd be perfect for that…and it wouldn't take me that long to learn electric guitar. I mean there's only a couple of chords in metal, isn't there?

What?

Of course …I'm sorry…you're in a hurry and here I am chewing your ear off about my career.

What was your order, again? That's right…

Do you want fries with that?

THE CHRISTMAS FAIRY

Adele Lewin and Nigel Palfreman

(Female, 50+)

Oh! Hello! You've caught me in the act I'm afraid – just trying to doll meself up a bit before the shop opens. There, finished. How do I look? This skirt looks alright, doesn't it? I found it on the rack. It's better than my old torn one. My backside doesn't look too big, does it? No, no…don't tell me. I don't want to know.

My name's Crystal. And as you can see – well, I hope you can see – I'm a Christmas Fairy. You know, the Christmas Fairy that sits on top of the Christmas tree. At least, I used to sit on top of the Christmas tree! Now, I just sit on top of the shelf in this Op Shop.

Well, it's Christmas Eve. To be honest though, it just doesn't feel like Christmas to me 'cos I'm still stuck here. Five years I've been here. Five years! I want a family to love me again - a family I can make happy. Like I used to with the Jones', before they told me that it was time for me to hang up my wings and stuck me in a box with Nat King Cole and Bing Crosby. They'd bought another fairy see, one younger than me. Usurped I was – just 'cos I'd lost me blush of youth. Well, that and me wings were getting a bit bent and me hair had lost its sparkles. It didn't matter that I'd been with them for years. They still dumped me. I saw her once, just before they shut the lid on me. She looked like a right old tart – brassy blonde hair, and a gossamer silk dress so sheer it left nothing to the imagination!

I forgive them though, I do, but…it still makes me a bit teary every time I think of it. But that's life I suppose – out with the old, in with the new. But you've got to look forward haven't you?

Now I want a new family. I want a new family to put me on top of their Christmas tree and say: "Oooh, she soooo beautiful." And I want to see all the kids opening their presents on Christmas morning and seeing their little faces all aglow, and then seeing them squabble with each other about who's got the biggest or the best ones! And I want to hear old Granny farting away because 'cos she's eaten too many brussels sprouts, and then see the kids holding their noses and hear them shouting: "Poooooaaa! Granny's let one off again. Quick, someone get the gas masks!"

And then…and THEN…I want to hear Michael Bublé singing White Christmas – oooh, that voice, it makes my loins go all tingly! Well don't look so shocked. A fairy has her urges as well you know.

Look, I know I shouldn't complain – at least I've got a roof over me head. And I've got me mates here and we do try to keep each other company, 'specially at Christmas 'cos it gets so lonely. But…well…it's just not the same as being in a family. And, as long as I'm in this Op Shop I'm not fulfilling my raison d'etre – you know, making people happy.

But I haven't given up hope. Do you know, every year when I see someone I like the look of looking at the Christmas things I take a deep breath, squeeze me eyes tight, wiggle me wand a bit (can't wiggle it too hard 'cos it's on its last legs already) and send out positive vibrations: "Buuuy me. Buuuy me." And it seems to work because they suddenly turn around, look at me, pick me up, smile, and I think, 'This is it! This is really it! They're gonna' buy me. I'm gonna' go to a home again and be loved again and be useful again!' And then… THEN…they always spot some younger fairy on the shelf. A fairy who's still got her looks, and her sparkly hair, and her wings all fluttery – not all bent like mine. I know its hard to believe, but I used to be young and beautiful, and my hair used to be sparkly. And my wand…my wand was a wonder to behold!

The truth is nobody loves a fairy when she's forty.

(Sings)

Nobody loves a fairy when she's forty
Nobody loves a fairy when she's old
She may still have a magic power but that is not enough
They like their bit of magic from a younger bit of stuff
When once your silver star has lost its glitter
And your tinsel looks like rust instead of gold
Fairy days are ending when your wand has started bending
No-one loves a fairy when she's old.

But…this year I might just be in luck, 'cos I'm the only Christmas fairy in the shop…

But hang on tic, I thought that last year …and then, at the very last minute, in waltzes this fairy like she's Dame Nellie Melba, wearing a great big hooded cape. And she looks at me and she says, "I'm Kylie, and I've just arrived. But I have no doubt that by tonight I shall be in the home of a wonderful family sitting on top of their Christmas tree." Her face looked vaguely familiar but I just couldn't place her. Anyway, she starts rattling on about how bea-u-ti-ful everyone thinks she is and how every-body wants her.

So I said to her, I said, 'Well, you might not believe this looking at me now but once upon a time I was the crème de la crème of Christmas fairies and everybody wanted me.' Well it's true. I used to sit on the top of the Christmas tree in Harrods. Knightsbridge. People would come from far and wide just to marvel at my beauty as I sat there in all me glory. I never let it go to my head though. I maintained my humility in the midst of adoration. I mean, that's what a Christmas fairy does when she's By Appointment to Her Majesty The Queen.'

Anyway, what I didn't say to Dame Nellie was that one fateful day I was snapped up by Lord and Lady Arbuthnot of Aberdeen. I thought I was going to have pride of place on their Christmas tree. But no. They gave me to their cook! Their cook for gawd's sake! For services rendered. And she… she sent me to her cousin in Australia! Australia! Who in their right mind goes to AUSTRALIA? No offence.

I was in shock. It took me weeks to recover.

But…then…I learned to love my Jones'. And my Jones' loved me. For ten years they loved me. And then, just 'cos I lost me looks – I mean we all lose our looks in the end don't we – they dumped me in this Op Shop.

I know what you're thinking. You're thinking 'it can't be all that bad in an Op Shop.' Well, see how you'd like it if you were here. You'd have kids grabbing you by the arms swinging you around their heads; lifting up your skirt to have peek at your privates. And not just the kids neither. It's humiliating!

Anyway, back to Dame Nellie Melba…

She obviously hadn't been listening to a word I said and she starts going on about her last family, the Jones', and how she was the favourite fairy of Becky Jones. I thought 'Becky Jones'… It couldn't be…

Then I began to twig where I'd seen that face before. So I said to her, 'Why don't you take your cape off and make yourself comfy.' She says, "I'm fine the way I am thanks." So I says, "Oh go on. You must be hot in that beautiful cape." "No," she says. So I grabs it, and I'm tugging and she's pulling, and

I'm tugging again and she's pulling again, and then I'm tugging again, and suddenly it off. And there it is…brassy blond hair, and a gossamer thin dress showing everything god gave her. I said, 'It's you. You're the one who nicked my Jones'. You're the reason the Jones' dumped me.' "Well what if I am," she says, "It's not my fault the Jones' chose me, with my stunning looks and beautiful hair, over a drab old fuddy-duddy relic of a fairy like you!" 'Ooooh!' I said, 'You're just a fake and a phoney. A bit of plastic fantastic, with no depth and no respect for character!' "Listen DEARIE," she says, "you lost your sparkle and was disposed of. But me, I'll always Sparkle." And then she waltzes off to find the best spot in the display window.

Well, I just lost it. All my misery hit me all at once. Losing the Jones'. Being stuck here for five years and being so lonely. And, not being able to make people happy.

Eh, hang on a minute. There's someone over there I like the look of…

Buuuuuuy me! Buuuuuuy me!

Wish me luck!

ALWAYS THE BRIDESMAID

Nigel Palfreman

(Female, 25+)

(Vicky - a twenty - something young girl, usually fun & bubbly - is walking home after a one night stand. She walks past a park bench, stops and then sits.)

It's sad isn't it. You'd have thought that in this day and age, chivalry would be alive and well. That boys would, you know offer to give you a lift home or something, I know its early. *(Looks at her watch)* 6.30am. Ok…fair enough he's probably still over the limit, but at least get me a cab or an über. But no, 15 minutes ago he gets up, goes to the bathroom, comes back in the room, throws my dress at me and says 'Righto, time to move on!' That was it. That blunt. No Niceties, No 'Look Vicky, I had a really great time it was nice and all that and we had fun but, but look, maybe you should...listen do you want me to call a cab?' No, just 'Righto, time to move on!' He didn't even ask for my number. To be honest, I don't even think he knew my name.

He wasn't like that last night. He was sweet, we talked, he bought me a drink.

He walked up to me all confident, I like confident you know. Kind of shows they're not intimidated. I was with Ella and all my girlfriends, which for someone who doesn't know us can be pretty intimidating. Ella's full of confidence you know, laughing and joking. She can take the piss out of anyone, really cut you to the bone. Could be your hair, the way you talk, where you're from. If you're a north sider forget it. A bad influence, that's what my Dad used to say about her, and that was when we were in Year 5. 12 years later and we're still as close as ever, doing each other's makeup, going shopping together, annoying my little brother, going out clubbing and holding back each other's hair over the toilet. So I can imagine that Ollie, that's last night's name, would feel a bit intimidated to come over. But over he came, full of confidence.

"Excuse me, would you mind if I bought you a drink?"

"Yeah sure of course."

"Fantastic."

And it all started from there. We drank, we talked, we laughed. We danced. Now, I love a guy that can dance. He doesn't have to be a great dancer, although that is...pretty hot…gets your juices going. That's what Ella would say. Just someone that gives it a go, you know. Then before you know it, I'm in the back of a cab with him heading for his house. A few drinks later and 'wham bam thank you ma'am'. He's passed out and I'm lying there thinking, wasn't the best shag I've had, but he is really nice. This could be the start of something. Admittedly I was pretty pissed myself but there was that little sliver of optimism. Good looking guy, funny, sweet, can chat, can dance, all the boxes ticked. Then 15 minutes ago - "Righto, time to move on'.

Bastard!

I'd be lying if I said it wasn't the first time this had happened. I seem to attract the one-night stand crowd. It's ok, if you're up for a bit of fun then its fine, but despite Ella's confidence, bravado and filthy mouth, I want what she's got. A guy who cares about her, would do anything for her, treats her like she's the only person in the world. Goes out on the piss with her, loves watching her have fun with her friends and doesn't mind if she has too much to drink and vomits everywhere - or at least doesn't show that he minds. I want that warm cosy feeling, to feel safe and loved. I can't understand why I can't find love. Fair enough, you're not likely to find love at Mooseheads on a Thursday night. But the shows on TV like Farmer Wants a Wife or adverts on the socials for Bumble and eHarmony and that, make it look easy to find love, your soul mate, life partner. The only thing I found online was slight case of chlamydia, and the antibiotics soon cleared that up. I'm kidding, I'm kidding, it just burned a bit when I went to pee, that's all.

I do seem to be unlucky in love though. Not wanting to blow my own trumpet but I'm alright looking, all the right things in all the right places. Somethings could be a little bigger, other things a little smaller. I admit I'm not perfect, I am quite normal. I'm not a lunatic, psycho girlfriend.

Shelley, mine and Ella's mate, is a little bit mental when it comes to boys. As soon as she met Pete, she was planning the next 5 years of her life.

'Well, we'll be going to the Gold Coast for our 4 month anniversary and then when we get back we're going to be looking at a flat, somewhere near the center of town. It'll be so cool because you guys will be able to stay there when we all go out. He'll probably be going out with his friends - hey maybe we can set you up with one of Pete's friends Vick, that'll be awesome. Then after a year or two I think we'll probably get engaged and maybe think about moving out to the suburbs. Can't party you whole life can you Vick?'

She's crazy but her and Pete are still together and happy. I don't know if I want her intensity. She is loopy but I do want that Sunday morning cuddle.

I thought I found it a year or so ago. I met James.

We met at a club, bit like Ollie really, he was confident but he was fit. I don't just mean good looking, he was ripped. He had these massive arms, legs like barrels and washboard stomach, Oh my God, it was amazing running your fingers down his stomach. His body was awesome! Well, most of it was awesome. If I'm honest, there were some small issues with his body. He was er, more of a grower than a show-er, down there, if you know what I mean, and it didn't really grow that much. Sex was still pretty good, early on I did ask him if he took steroids but promised me he didn't and everything was 'Just as God intended'. Not entirely sure if God intended things to be that compact but you can't have everything can you.

James was lovely, a nice guy, trained a lot in the gym, and for sport, but then little things started to get on my nerves. Not that little thing..other stuff, stupid stuff. Like, he loves the footy shows. Now, I can take or leave football but not those idiots. You know, the ones who used play and think it was a better game when they did…they are idiots. Actually, they are dicks…big ones!

I suppose I could have forgiven him for the footy, but then there was Campbell's Chunky Beef and Veg Soup.

You know how when one tiny little insignificant thing can get on your nerves and start to wind you up. It doesn't matter what else they do, they could be bloody Mother Theresa for all it matters, but that little thing, just grates on you, builds up and up and up and up, until you just can't stand it any longer and things come to a head. Well, in mine and James's case it led to us splitting up after a couple of months. It should've been the honeymoon period, can't keep our hands off each other, hugging and kissing all the time and it would've been, but for Campbell's bloody Chunky Beef and Veg Soup. This is going to sound so petty now, but … for lunch he slurped the soup. Not just a little slurp but a full on *sluuuuurp*, the kind of slurp my Grandad would've been proud of drinking his tea. I couldn't stand it, all I could think about was the bloody slurping, having a beer, slurp, having some food, slurp, even when he was kissing me. Slurp slurp slurp. I had to end it. It was doing my head in. Poor James and his incredible, incredible body.

Dumped over his lunchtime soup.

Maybe I deserve it. Maybe I deserve the arseholes who treat me like shit. Idiots like Brad who called his dick the Truth, because

'Vicky, you can't handle the Truth'. Or Kevin who was a bit of player and told me that I was like all the other girls he'd been with 'Same wine, different bottle.'

You know what though, I don't want to be second best, I don't to be treated like I'm a piece of scrap paper, picked up then tossed on the floor. I'm better than that. You know what, fuck you Brad with your penile nicknames and fuck you Kev with your perfect teeth and shit pick up lines. And fuck you Ollie, you may have forgotten my name, kicked me out of your house and not got me cab, but as much as it pains me to say it you were right. Righto, time to move on. Move on from you, move on from Kev, Brad and all the other self-obsessed tossers and go find someone who will treat me well. Someone who will look after me, someone who will laugh with me, someone who will hold my hand, someone who will dance with me, someone who will drink with me, someone who will hold back my hair while I vomit in the toilet, someone who will cuddle me on a Sunday morning and someone, someone who will love me. Someone like...

(Vicky takes her phone from her bag and makes a call).

"Er James hi, it's Vicky. Look sorry for calling so early, bit of a rough night, you know. And I'm sorry for not calling you a while back when things went you know, I um, it's a long story. Listen, I was wondering if you want to get together, meet up or something? You know a bite to

eat, something like that, breakfast not lunch. I'm sorry and I...miss you. Anyway, let me know what you think. Hope to speak to you soon. Bye."

Fingers crossed.

(*Vicky's phone rings. She looks at who's calling and smiles).*

Hi James...

CONTRIBUTORS

Kirsty Budding

Kirsty is a writer, producer and actress based in Canberra, Australia. Kirsty has a background in writing and producing for the stage, winning a number of local awards including the Canberra Area Theatre Award for Best Original Work for The Fairytale Channel and the Short+Sweet Festival Best Script Award for Brexit. She was the 2018 Winner of the ACT Writing and Publishing Award for Fiction for her debut anthology Paper Cuts: Comedic and Satirical Monologues for Audition or Performance.

Harriet Elvin

Harriet Elvin is a Canberra-based playwright. Her plays are often performed in short play festivals in Canberra and Sydney, and are regularly featured on ArtSound Radio Theatre. Apart from on stage and radio, Harriet's plays have been performed in venues as varied as the Commonwealth Club, Smiths Alternative Bookshop, and Muse restaurant. She has also directed short plays and judged short play festivals, and her other writing interests include short stories and poetry. After a long career in arts management, Harriet is now at the ANU Research School of Management, studying how arts organisations address competing creative and financial goals.

Adele Lewin

Since training full time at London Academy of Music and Dramatic Art, Adele has worked extensively as a professional actress in theatre, film, television and radio, performing a diverse range of roles. She's also written, and performed two other monologues, Love and Girl's Night Out at the Street Theatre and the Depot Theatre Sydney. The Christmas Fairy is the first piece Adele's co-written, finding it a wonderful experience, incorporating Nigel's and her own ideas to produce a monologue which is both touching and amusing. Writing The Christmas Fairy also gave Adele the opportunity to comment on the reality behind the glitter of Christmas, a reality experienced by many.

John Lombard

John is a playwright, actor, arts journalist, producer, comedian and occasional burlesque performer. His play The Literary Monogamist won the People's Choice Award at Short+Sweet Canberra 2014, and his play The Bell Coffin was performed on Radio National's program Radiotonic. He started Canberra's pun slam Capital Punishment, has written arts reviews for Canberra Critics' Circle, and has acted for Lakespeare and Canberra REP. He writes a story every month for his podcast, A Crisp Moment of Unease.

Bart Meehan

Bart is a writer, editor and producer/broadcaster. He has had short plays and monologues produced for stage throughout Australia and internationally. He is the host of ArtSound Radio Theatre. The Pursuit of Art won The Logues 2024, run by Canberra Repertory Theatre.

Nigel Palfreman

Nigel is a playwright, actor, director, producer, and occasional film maker. Nigel has had his work performed around Australia, London, Dubai, Los Angeles and Mumbai. He has been nominated for best scriptwriting awards but has not won any…yet. He willl keep plugging away. When Nigel is not writing, he teaches Drama and Media at a school in Canberra as well as directing and producing some of the schools plays.

Judith Petersen

Judith Peterson has been involved in the Canberra film and theatre scene for over 10 years. She reignited her love for acting in her 40's and started her own small production company "Allycat Productions" that has produced theatre and films with a wonderful team of locals.

Milton Keynes UK
Ingram Content Group UK Ltd.
UKHW021329280724
446040UK00008B/84